THE ULTIMATE BOOK OF
DANGEROUS
ANIMALS

THE ULTIMATE BOOK OF DANGEROUS ANIMALS

THE ULTIMATE BOOK OF DANGEROUS INSECTS

THE ULTIMATE BOOK OF DANGEROUS JOBS

THE ULTIMATE BOOK OF DANGEROUS PLACES

THE ULTIMATE BOOK OF DANGEROUS SPORTS & ACTIVITIES

THE ULTIMATE BOOK OF DANGEROUS WEATHER

THE ULTIMATE BOOK OF

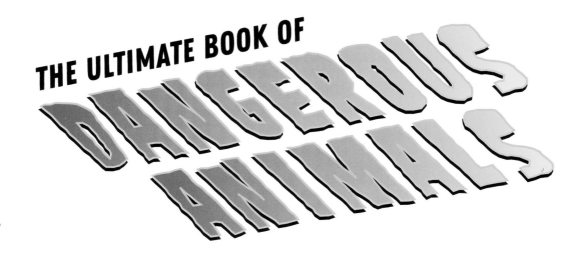

DANGEROUS ANIMALS

H.W. POOLE

MASON CREST
PHILADELPHIA · MIAMI

Mason Crest
450 Parkway Drive, Suite D
Broomall, Pennsylvania 19008
(866) MCP-BOOK (toll-free)
www.masoncrest.com

Copyright © 2020 by Mason Crest, an imprint of National Highlights, Inc. All rights reserved. No part of this publication may be reproduced or transmitted in any form or by any means, electronic or mechanical, including photocopying, recording, taping, or any information storage and retrieval system, without permission from the publisher.

First printing
9 8 7 6 5 4 3 2 1

ISBN (hardback) 978-1-4222-4225-4
ISBN (series) 978-1-4222-4224-7
ISBN (ebook) 978-1-4222-7582-5

Cataloging-in-Publication Data on file with the Library of Congress.

Developed and Produced by National Highlights Inc.
Editor: Peter Jaskowiak
Interior and cover design: Annemarie Redmond
Production: Michelle Luke

CONTENTS

KEY ICONS TO LOOK FOR:

 Words to Understand: These words with their easy-to-understand definitions will increase the reader's understanding of the text, while building vocabulary skills.

 Sidebars: This boxed material within the main text allows readers to build knowledge, gain insights, explore possibilities, and broaden their perspectives by weaving together additional information to provide realistic and holistic perspectives.

 Educational Videos: Readers can view videos by scanning our QR codes, providing them with additional educational content to supplement the text. Examples include news coverage, moments in history, speeches, iconic sports moments, and much more!

 Research Projects: Readers are pointed toward areas of further inquiry connected to each chapter. Suggestions are provided for projects that encourage deeper research and analysis.

 Series Glossary of Key Terms: This back-of-the-book glossary contains terminology used throughout the series. Words found here increase the reader's ability to read and comprehend higher-level books and articles in this field.

SERIES INTRODUCTION

The *Ultimate Danger* set explores hair-raising hobbies, crime-ridden cities, death-dealing hurricanes, and much more. But what makes something dangerous?

The answer may depend on your perspective. For example, some people would say that guns are so inherently dangerous that having one in the house is unthinkable. But to those who feel comfortable around guns, it's fine to have weapons in the house—even desirable!—as long as they're stored properly. Or consider this: most Americans think of New Zealand as a faraway land with breathtaking scenery and . . . who knows, maybe surfing? The point is, Americans don't know all that much about New Zealand, and it looks adorably harmless to us from so far away. But to New

SOME INFORMATION ON INFORMATION BOXES

Each entry in this set includes an information box that provides basic facts about that topic. Most are self-explanatory, but a few require a little bit of explanation.

In *Dangerous Animals*, one category is called "IUCN Red List." This refers to a database created by the International Union for Conservation of Nature (IUCN). The IUCN assesses the population levels of animal species, and also whether that population is growing or declining. Each species is given a designation, such as "Endangered," "Vulnerable," or, if it's doing well, "Least Concern."

The *Dangerous Places* volume has chapters on dangerous cities and countries—both use population information from the World Population Review website. Almost by definition, the countries and cities covered here tend to be unstable, meaning good data can be difficult to come by. In addition, some countries don't report trustworthy numbers, and movements of refugees can shift population levels rapidly.

In the "Dangerous Countries" chapter, the information box also gives travel advisory information from the U.S. State Department, which assesses the safety (or lack thereof) of countries to help tourists decide whether or not to visit them. Countries are put into four categories, with increasing levels of danger:

- Level 1 (exercise normal precautions)
- Level 2 (exercise increased caution)
- Level 3 (reconsider travel)
- Level 4 (do not travel)

Zealand's indigenous Maori population, who were robbed and oppressed during two hundred years of imperialist rule, New Zealand may not seem quite as adorable.

Given all that, it's clear that "dangerous" is subjective. The term can also be a vaguely insulting one in some contexts. Consider the people of St. Louis, a city frequently included on lists of "most dangerous cities" due to its high rate of violent crimes per citizen. Many residents are annoyed about the city they love ending up on those lists. They'll hold forth passionately about how the statistics are misreported, misunderstood, and just generally unfair.

But not everyone finds "dangerous" to be insulting—for some, the word indicates something that's a heck of a lot of fun. Three of this set's six volumes (*Dangerous Jobs, Dangerous Places*, and *Dangerous Sports & Activities*) are partly or entirely devoted to dangers that humans *actively pursue*. Even those of us who would rather not dance with actual danger can't get enough of TV shows and films that scare us, startle us, and let us experience danger at a distance. Some of us even read (and write!) books about the topic. So, without further ado, let's check out the *ultimate* in dangerous creatures, activities, and events.

WORDS TO UNDERSTAND

anaphylaxis: a type of severe and potentially fatal allergic reaction

carrion: dead animal flesh

emaciated: dangerously thin due to lack of food

gore: to stab with a horn or tusk

hierarchical: a community or group that is organized by rank

MRSA: acronym for the bacteria, Methicillin-resistant *Staphylococcus aureus*

staph: short for *staphylococcus aureus*, a type of bacteria

undulate: to move in a wave-like motion

CHAPTER 1

DANGEROUS MAMMALS

Whether it's "trampled by an elephant," "torn apart by a lion," or "mauled by a bear," who can resist a good "when mammals attack" story? Almost nobody.

But before we dive into the wild world of ferocious mammals, it's worth noting that the most dangerous mammals on Earth won't be found behind the bars of any zoo. No, the most dangerous ones by far will be found on the other side of the bars. Because, yes, the most dangerous mammal is us—all 7.6 billion of us humans.

In 2018 the National Academy of Sciences announced its finding that humans, while making up only 0.01 percent of life on this planet, have managed to wipe out about 80 percent of our fellow mammals. Of all the mammals currently living on Earth, 60 percent are livestock, 36 percent are human, and only a paltry 4 percent are wild.

Lions and tigers and bears might be dangerous, but, in the end, wild mammals have much more to fear from human mammals than we do from them.

AFRICAN ELEPHANT

Scientific Name:
Loxodonta africana

Range: 37 countries in Africa

Diet: Grass, roots, bark, fruit

Life Span: About 70 years

IUCN Red List: Vulnerable

African elephants are not just the biggest land mammals on Earth: they are also one of the smartest. Researchers have learned that elephants can communicate with one another, use tools, and even understand human language.

Elephant communities are very **hierarchical**. Males struggle for dominance, and their interactions can get quite violent. In addition to their massive size, elephants are armed with very strong tusks that can stab and slash. And while their diet is strictly vegetarian, elephants won't hesitate to defend themselves against lions or other predators—and that includes humans. According to one estimate, about 500 people are killed by African elephants every year.

Male elephants are most dangerous to humans during a period called *musth*, when they go searching for mates. An elephant experiencing musth may attack anyone or anything that appears to be a threat. Female elephants, on the other hand, are most likely to become aggressive if they feel their young are in danger. (You'd be extremely protective, too, if you had to be pregnant for 22 months!)

An average of 500 deaths per year might sound like a lot, but it's worth noting that humans kill about 55 African elephants *per day.* Hunting and poaching have reduced the population of African elephants from several million down to only about 400,000. Their tusks, which are so important for self-defense, are made of ivory, which is prized on the global black market.

If you are fortunate enough to encounter elephants in the wild, don't assume that just because they are big, they are very slow. Elephants are surprisingly fast when they want to be—for short sprints, they can run approximately 15 mph (24 kph), and possibly faster. That means you probably can't outrun one! If you really get into trouble with an elephant, the best advice is to climb a tree as quickly as possible.

The American business executive Tom Siebel told *Forbes* magazine about being attacked by an elephant while he was on safari in Tanzania in 2009:

> *It knocked me to the ground with its trunk, it rolled me, punched me, put a tusk through my left thigh, gored it, then ripped it out sideways. It stepped on my leg, kicked my leg, broke six ribs and ripped up my shoulder. . . . Imagine what it's like taking an elephant tusk through the thigh or hav[ing] a 6-ton animal step on your leg. It just snaps. The pain was intolerable.*

BEARS

There are eight species of bear, and they all present potential danger to humans. (Yes, even the super-cuddly panda should not be messed with!) But two species in particular are designed for maximum havoc.

GRIZZLY BEAR

Scientific Name:
Ursus arctos horribilis

Range: Western Canada, northwestern United States, Alaska

Diet: Plants, insects, some meat

Life Span: 20–25 years

IUCN Red List: Least Concern

On good days, grizzly bears are shy plant-eaters with no interest in humans. In general, grizzlies would much rather eat their weight in moth larvae than bother with people. But if a grizzly feels threatened, or if a mama grizzly feels her cubs are threatened—then watch out.

Grizzlies can sprint very fast, up to 35 mph (56 kph)—an angry grizzly could easily chase down even an Olympic-level runner. They have 4-inch claws that are ideal for ripping flesh. And, contrary to rumor, they *are* able to climb trees if they truly want to. Grizzlies aren't eager to climb, like their black bear cousins are, but they'll do it if they have a good reason. And you *don't* want that reason to be you.

POLAR BEAR

Scientific Name:
Ursus maritimus

Range: The Arctic
(including Alaska, Canada,
Russia, Greenland)

Diet: Meat (usually seal)

Life Span: 25–35 years

IUCN Red List:
Vulnerable

Weighing as much as a grand piano, polar bears are built for hunting down prey. Unlike grizzlies, polar bears eat meat exclusively. After all, there aren't a lot of vegetarian options in the frozen north. Fortunately, when times are good, polar bears are much more interested in hunting seals than hunting people.

But times are not so good for polar bears these days. Habitat loss has left increasing numbers of polar bears dangerously short of food, and that can spell trouble. In 2010, two napping Norwegian campers were attacked by a polar bear. The bear dragged one of the campers right out of his tent and across the ice. The following year, an **emaciated** polar bear killed a teenage British tourist and injured several others in the tour group. Experts worry that these attacks may become more frequent in the future, as polar bears are forced into increased contact with human settlements.

CHECK IT OUT!

Is there a zoo in your area? What dangerous mammals live there? If you can visit, try to find out what special strategies the zookeepers use to keep themselves safe.

BLACK RHINOCEROS

Scientific Name:
Diceros bicornis

Range: Southern and eastern Africa

Diet: Plants

Life Span: 40–50 years

IUCN Red List:
Critically Endangered

There are five species of rhinoceros—some live in the Far East, some in India. They are all large and very powerful, but most of them are pretty shy. It's Africa's black rhinoceros that has earned the most fearsome reputation.

Black rhinos have two horns and very thick hides, and they can weigh as much as 3,000 pounds (1,370 kg). They have poor eyesight, smaller-than-average brains, and aggressive personalities. Fortunately, even ill-tempered black rhinos tend to be solitary, and attacks on humans are not very common.

The most likely way you'd get into trouble with a rhino is if a female thinks you intend to harm her young in some way. Rhinos only reproduce every 2.5 to 5 years, and they only have one baby at a time. Mothers are extremely protective, and they won't hesitate to charge a person, a jeep, or another rhino if they sense a threat.

At South Africa's Mountain Zebra National Park in 2012, a warden stumbled upon a female rhino who had just given birth. The rhino **gored** the warden, who ended up in the hospital with chest and stomach injuries.

CAPE BUFFALO

Scientific Name: *Syncerus caffer*

Range: Central and Southern Africa

Diet: Plants

Life Span: About 20 years

IUCN Red List: Least Concern

Cape buffalo (or African buffalo) may look like hipster cows, but they are arguably the most dangerous animals in Africa. With their compact, powerful bodies and massive horns, these creatures can flip over cars, toss lions into the air, and trample humans to death under their great bulk. It's no surprise, then, that African hunters refer to Cape buffalo as "the Widowmaker."

Several factors make the Cape buffalo especially deadly. Start with those large horns: spanning about 3 feet (1 m) across, buffalo use them against predators, prey, and even each other when necessary. They are also massive—males weigh about 1,300 pounds (590 kg)—and they're *fast*, chasing down prey at 35 mph (57 kph).

Cape Buffalo travel in herds, and they support one another. If one member of a herd is attacked, the others will come to its aid. A hunter bringing down one buffalo may find himself surrounded by a crowd of its angry friends. What's more, Cape buffalo are not only smart, but also eerily patient. An injured buffalo will often stalk the hunter or predator who hurt them—even if it takes *years*. According to Lindsay Hunt, a conservationist in South Africa, "The adage, 'an elephant never forgets' would be matched by 'a buffalo never forgives.'"

This video of Cape buffalo in action proves how dangerous they can be.

DOMESTIC DOG

Scientific Name:
Canis lupus familiaris

Range: Global

Diet: Commercial dog food, human scraps

Life Span: Roughly 10 years (depending on breed)

IUCN Red List: Not assessed

Approximately 4.7 million Americans are bitten by dogs every year, and roughly half of the victims are kids. Most bites are fairly minor (although even a "minor" bite is not an enjoyable experience!). Every year, around 350,000 Americans are bitten severely enough that they have to visit the emergency room, and one study counted 433 dog-bite fatalities between 2005 and 2017.

Dogs can carry a viral disease called rabies, which is 100 percent fatal in humans if left untreated. Fortunately, rabies is rare in North America, but unfortunately, it is widespread in developing countries. Globally, rabies kills almost 60,000 people every year. According to the World Health Organization, dogs are responsible for 99 percent of human rabies cases.

INFECTIONS AND DOG BITES

In addition to rabies, dog bites bring a number of other health risks. Tetanus (or lockjaw) is a serious infection contracted through skin punctures. Dogs can also carry other types of bacteria that cause infections, including *Pasteurella* and *Capnocytophaga*. A very dangerous condition called *sepsis* can occur when bacteria in an infected bite causes an immune reaction in the victim's bloodstream.

Another risk is **MRSA**. MRSA is a type of **staph** infection that is difficult to treat because the bacteria that causes it has become resistant to antibiotics. MRSA travels easily between dogs and humans. According to the Centers for Disease Control and Prevention (CDC), as MRSA becomes more common in humans, it also becomes more common in dogs.

GREY WOLF

Scientific Name:
Canis lupus

Range: North America, Europe, Asia

Diet: Moose, caribou, deer, elk, occasionally livestock or carrion

Life Span: 6–8 years

IUCN Red List: Least Concern

Whether it's "Little Red Riding Hood," "Peter and the Wolf," or "The Three Little Pigs," the appearance of a wolf in a children's story is a strong hint that somebody is about to come to a bad end. These stories have roots in the long, bloody history of human–wolf interaction. In days past, when grazing animals like sheep were a vital part of agriculture— and when, remember, children frequently worked as shepherds—wolves posed a real and present danger. A French historian managed to count almost 7,600 deaths due to wolves from 1362 to 1918—and that was in his country alone.

Today, things have changed, and wolves pose a far more limited threat to human populations. Wolf populations have been greatly reduced due to hunting and habitat loss. However, in recent years, some populations have rebounded, and that may mean more violent encounters as wolves and humans compete for

the same resources. In 2010 a woman was killed while jogging near Chignik Lake, Alaska; the tracks of multiple wolves were found in the snow around her body.

In 2012 a medical journal reported a grim case. A 60-year-old man in rural Turkey had been sitting in his garden when a rabid wolf sprang from the woods, jumped on him, and bit his face. Amazingly, the man was able to strangle the wolf to death despite his severe injuries. Tragically, he later died in the hospital from rabies.

HIPPOPOTAMUS

Scientific Name:
Hippopotamus amphibius

Range: Eastern Africa

Diet: Grass and some aquatic plants

Life Span: 40–50 years

IUCN Red List: Vulnerable

These massive "river horses" are the lovable stars of an uncountable number of children's books and cartoons. But what if you are, let's say, a fisherman in Senegal? Then hippos aren't lovable at all. In fact, one man who fishes the Gambia River told a reporter that hippos are "evil monsters who attack us night and day." In fact, hippos are considered by many to be the most dangerous land animal in Africa.

A few factors combine to make hippos especially lethal. Their large size and weight are obviously major factors, as are their sharp and powerful teeth. Hippos are also very territorial, and as humans encroach more and more on their territory, they don't hesitate to fight back. They are also adept both in the water and out of it—they can smash boats and drag people under the water, or simply trample them to death on land.

PABLO'S HIPPOS

As "dangerous mammals" go, the Colombian drug kingpin Pablo Escobar ranked fairly high in his day—it's been estimated that he was directly or indirectly responsible for the deaths of more than 7,000 people. On his massive estate, called *Hacienda Napoles,* Escobar created a private zoo, with giraffes, ostriches, antelopes, and, yes, hippos.

When Escobar was finally killed, in 1993, the estate was taken over by the Colombian government. Most of the exotic animals were sent elsewhere. Nobody ever moved the hippos, though. Some still live at the hacienda, while others escaped its confines and now live freely in the rivers and lakes of Colombia.

HYENA

Scientific Name: *Crocuta crocuta*

Range: Africa, south of the Sahara Desert

Diet: Meat

Life Span: 8 years (females), 4 years (males) in the wild; 12 years in captivity

IUCN Red List: Least Concern

GIRLS VERSUS BOYS

Spotted hyenas live in hierarchical clans with anywhere from 5 to 80 members. Females are physically larger than males, and they hold a higher social position. A clan's lowest-ranking female hyena still ranks higher than any male. What's more, males are not able to challenge other males to improve their status—they only move up when other males die. Scientists don't know why hyena clans have such a strict social order. We do know that it takes a toll on the males, who only live half as long as females.

There are several species of hyena, but when people talk about this distant relative of the dog, they are usually referring to the spotted hyena. Spotted hyenas are also called "laughing" hyenas—because of the evil-sounding giggles they make. People who live near hyenas tend to hate them because they kill a lot of livestock. But it's myth that hyenas only eat dead animals or human corpses. While they do eat some **carrion**, hyenas are impressive hunters and can take down prey far larger than themselves.

Because they resemble dogs, you might not realize just how big spotted hyenas can be—they grow to almost 6 feet (2 m) long and weigh up to 180 pounds (82 kg). Hyenas hunt antelopes, zebras, gazelles, wildebeests, and even small hippos. Their large stomachs can hold more than 30 lbs (16 kg) of meat at a time—this enables them to go for several days without eating.

JAGUAR

Scientific Name:
Panthera onca

Range: Central and
South America, Mexico

Diet: Meat

Life Span: 10–15
years in wild; 20 years in
captivity

IUCN Red List: Near
Threatened

South America's largest cat, the jaguar takes its name from the Tupi-Guanari language. The word *yaguar* can be translated as "kills with one leap." This name may have been inspired by the jaguar's tendency to hide in trees and ambush prey from above. Jaguars are extremely good hunters. They're fast, with a top speed of 50 mph (80 kph), and their jaws are so powerful that they can shatter a turtle's shell just by biting it. Jaguars are also excellent swimmers, catching fish and a small type of alligator called a caiman.

Jaguars used to live in southern parts of the United States, but no longer. Today, humans and jaguars are coming into increasing conflict, as South American ranches and plantations spread onto land where jaguars once hunted freely. Jaguars are more than able to kill and eat cows if they get the chance, which makes them the enemies of farmers and ranchers.

LION

Scientific Name:
Panthera leo

Range: Africa, mostly south of the Sahara Desert

Diet: Meat, including wildebeests, antelopes, zebras, and baboons

Life Span: About 10 years in the wild, as many as 25 years in captivity

IUCN Red List: Vulnerable

Unlike their fellow African animals the elephant and the hippo, which only attack humans when they feel threatened, lions will kill humans for food. We are not their first-choice meal, though! Lions vastly prefer zebras or wildebeests to humans. In total, lions kill an estimated 250 people per year.

But as you'll see again and again in these pages, lions are not nearly the threat to us that we are to them. About a hundred years ago, there were approximately 200,000 lions, scattered all over the African continent. Today, that number is down to around 23,000, and half of all lions live in a single country: Tanzania. Lions are killed by trophy hunters and by poachers, but the biggest problem is habitat loss. Land that used to belong to lion prides is increasingly being used for farming and ranching. Recently, some Tanzanian farmers have turned to poison, using chemistry to wipe out an entire pride in one go. If these trends continue, the African lion risks extinction by 2050.

PRIDES AND MANES

Lions are unique among all cats because they are social rather than solitary. They live in groups called *prides*, which can range in size from a handful to more than 30 members (about 15 is average).

Male lions are also the only cats with manes, and scientists believe that the social behavior and the manes are related. The larger and darker the mane, the more skilled a fighter the lion is thought to be, and the more female lions wish to breed with him.

SLOW LORIS

Scientific Name:
Nycticebus coucang

Range: Southeast Asia

Diet: Insects

Life Span: About 25 years

IUCN Red List: Vulnerable

Dangerous mammals usually make it their business to look as intimidating as possible. You can be forgiven, then, for looking at the slow loris and thinking, "That's dangerous? Nah…"

But, unlikely as it sounds, the slow loris is quite dangerous. This is due to venom stored in—wait for it—its armpit. When threatened, the loris licks itself, mixing the armpit poison with the saliva in its mouth. The venom from a single bite can cause **anaphylaxis** in humans and has, on occasion, been fatal.

Venom is usually a reptilian weapon—only a tiny number of mammals use it. Researchers theorize that the slow loris evolved its toxic defense strategy to mimic the cobras that share its habitat. Slow lorises even have an extra vertebra in their spinal columns, which makes it possible for them to **undulate** in a manner that's similar to the movement of cobras.

TIGER

Scientific Name: *Panthera tigris*

Range: Asia

Diet: Meat, including deer, monkeys, and civets

Life Span: 10–15 years in the wild; about 20 years in captivity

IUCN Red List: Endangered

The history of tiger and human interactions is long and bloody. A 2010 study attempted to count the total number of human deaths at the paws of tigers; their estimate was about 373,000 over a period of 200-plus years. That's a lot, but it's important to keep in mind that tiger attacks were a much bigger problem in the 19th century than they are now.

Alas, one reason for the decrease in tiger attacks is there are so few tigers left. In the early 1900s, there were approximately 100,000 tigers in the wild; in 2016, there were only some 3,800 left. However, there is reason for at least a little optimism: the number of tigers appears to be increasing (the previous count had been 3,200). Conservationists hope to see the numbers of tigers continue to increase.

WORDS TO UNDERSTAND

apex: the top of something; in this case, top of the food chain

dung: animal waste; manure

envenomate: the process by which venom is injected by means of a bite or sting

evolutionary biologist: a scientist who studies how species adapt and thrive over long periods of time

pituitary gland: a small organ at the base of the brain that releases important hormones

secrete: to release or discharge, usually refers to a liquid

superlative: describes something that is the top or most of something, such as largest or oldest

THE ULTIMATE BOOK OF DANGEROUS ANIMALS

CHAPTER 2

DANGEROUS REPTILES

Even in ancient times, reptiles loomed large in human storytelling. For example, the ultimate "bad guy" of Greek mythology was the god Typhon. Called "the father of all monsters," Typhon was a giant made entirely of snakes and dragons. Typhon's lover, Echidna, was another reptilian monster—half woman, half snake. And one of their children was the Hydra, a snake-monster that would famously regrow two new heads for every one that Hercules removed.

Evolutionary biologists suspect that there is a good reason for all this reptile-phobia. Early humans had to be constantly on guard against snake attacks, and a keen snake-detecting ability would have been a key survival skill. That means those who feared snakes lived longer, and therefore had more children, than those who didn't. Primates may have developed bigger brains and better vision *specifically* because of their need to avoid snakes. What's more, it's likely that snakes developed venom as a response to attacks from mammals.

Perhaps this ancient arms race explains why, from the devious serpent tempting Eve with an apple to Godzilla smashing downtown Tokyo, reptiles have a permanent place in our mental library of terrifying things.

ALLIGATOR

Scientific Name:
Alligator mississippiensis

Range: Southeastern United States

Diet: Fish, smaller reptiles, small mammals, and just about anything else

Life Span: 30–50 years

IUCN Red List: Least Concern

It's the sort of news story that chills the spine. On June 8, 2018, a woman was seen walking her dogs near a lake in Davie, Florida. A few hours later, the dogs were found alone, barking at the lake. Soon after, parts of the woman turned up in the belly of an alligator.

Alligators can be up to 15 feet (4.5 m) long and weigh as much as 1,000 pounds (450 kg). They lived alongside dinosaurs some 145 million years ago, as did their distant cousins, the crocodiles. But gators and crocs managed to survive, while dinosaurs were wiped

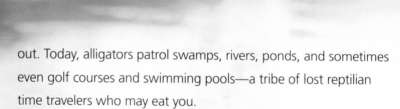

out. Today, alligators patrol swamps, rivers, ponds, and sometimes even golf courses and swimming pools—a tribe of lost reptilian time travelers who may eat you.

What is it that makes alligators so frightening? Is it their size? Their strength? Maybe it's their patience: gators can lie motionless in water for hours, remaining nearly invisible as they wait for prey to pass by. And when the moment arrives, alligators are alarmingly quick, slamming down their powerful jaws before their victims even know what's happening.

But while the first bite gets you, it's what happens next that ends you. When an alligator bites something that's bigger than it can swallow, it executes a move known as a *death roll*, spinning its body all the way around, over and over, to rip off hunks of flesh or even dismember its prey.

BLACK MAMBA

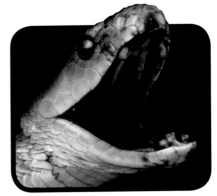

Scientific Name:
Dendroaspis polylepis

Range: Africa; especially common south of the Sahara, but has been seen as far north as Senegal

Diet: Small birds and mammals

Life Span: About 11 years

IUCN Red List: Least Concern

Africa's black mamba is a snake of many **superlatives**: it's the longest snake on the continent (up to 14 feet [4.2 m]); it slithers the fastest (over 12 mph [19 kph]); and its poison is one of the most lethal (without an antidote, death is certain in about 20 minutes). For all these reasons, the black mamba is often awarded with the ultimate superlative: world's deadliest snake.

While all that is true, black mambas are also extremely shy. They sincerely don't want to tangle with people if they can avoid it. They generally use their speed to flee from humans, not pursue them.

But if backed into a corner, the black mamba will rise to the challenge—literally! When threatened, the mamba lifts itself up, holding almost a third of its body in the air. If you find yourself facing off against a black mamba, you'll discover where the snake gets its name. You see, black mambas aren't actually black—their skin is dark green or grey. But if a black mamba attacks you, the last thing you'll see before it's too late is the deep black interior of its deadly mouth.

VENOMOUS OR POISONOUS?

You may hear people talk about "poisonous" snakes, but that usage is not quite correct: the terms *poisonous* and *venomous* refer to different things. Here's an easy way to remember the difference: a venomous animal makes you sick if it bites you; a poisonous animal makes you sick if you bite, eat, or touch it.

A black mamba, for example, is *venomous* but not *poisonous*. A Colorado River toad (see page 69), on the other hand, is *poisonous* but not *venomous*. That's because the toad doesn't bite; it **secretes** a poison on its skin.

BOOMSLANG

Scientific Name: *Dispholidus typus*

Range: Central and southern Africa

Diet: Small reptiles, frogs, birds' eggs

Life Span: About 8 years

IUCN Red List: Not assessed

Boomslang antivenom is on the World Health Organization's list of most essential medicines.

The boomslang is a member of a group of snakes called colubrids, whose fangs are in the backs of their mouths rather than in the front. Unlike the viper family (see page 42), most colubrids are not dangerous—they do have venom, but they can only deliver it in small, fairly weak amounts. One massive exception to this rule is the colubrid called the boomslang. Boomslangs live in the trees in central and southern Africa, where they grow to be between 3 and 6 feet long (about 1–2 m).

Boomslang venom is extremely dangerous—without treatment, death arrives, agonizingly, in about a day. Initial symptoms like nausea and vomiting, fever, and nosebleeds are followed by severe internal bleeding in the brain, lungs, and throughout the body. Fortunately, the slow-acting nature of the venom means there is time to get treatment. In addition to a dose of antivenom, bite victims may also require blood transfusions if they are to survive their boomslang encounters.

Find out what it's like to die of a boomslang bite.

CROCODILES

There are 14 different species of crocodile, and anybody who's seen *Peter Pan* knows better than to smile at any of them. But two species of crocodile are far more murderous than most.

NILE CROCODILE

Scientific Name: *Crocodylus niloticus*

Range: Sub-Saharan Africa, Nile River basin, Madagascar

Diet: Fish and anything else it can catch, from birds to zebras

Life Span: 45 years

IUCN Red List: Least Concern

Nile crocodiles are Africa's largest and most vicious freshwater predators. They grow much bigger than alligators—about 16 to 20 feet (5–6 m) long, and they can weigh as much as 1,650 pounds (750 kg). Most animals in this book will kill a human if threatened, but Nile crocodiles take it a step farther. These **apex** predators don't wait for something to threaten them: if they can catch it, it's lunch. Various estimates range from between 200 to 300 people killed by Nile crocs every year.

A cold-blooded hunter that's nearly as long as a soccer goal is wide—that's surely the stuff of nightmares. But Nile crocs do have one somewhat cuddly feature. They are the only crocodiles who actually take care of their young. Most female crocodilians lay their eggs and move on, but Nile moms not only stick around—they also fiercely protect their young from any predators.

SALTWATER CROCODILE

Scientific Name: *Crocodylus porosus*

Range: Southeast Asia, southern India, and northern Australia

Diet: Fish and crabs, birds, turtles, monkeys, foxes, wallabies

Life Span: 70 years

IUCN Red List: Least Concern

Some people dispute the Nile croc's position as the most dangerous crocodile; they argue that the saltwater croc is more bloodthirsty and even more likely to view human beings as takeout containers with legs.

Earlier we mentioned the alligator's death roll, which is used to pull large prey to pieces. Crocodiles can also roll, but their main strategy is to clamp down their jaws and drag prey under water, where they wait for the victim to drown. Sometimes "salties," as Australians call them, will do the death roll *after* the victim is dead, removing the limbs the way an experienced chef might carve up a turkey.

When it comes to striking fear in the hearts of their prey, you might think that saltwater crocodiles' giant jaws, powerful teeth, and death rolls would be enough. But you'd be wrong—crocs have one more trick up their scaly sleeves. They can leap, straight up in the air. They don't even need a running start; they use their back legs as springs.

GILA MONSTER

Scientific Name: *Heloderma suspectum*

Range: Southwestern United States

Diet: Small mammals and lizards, birds' eggs, insects, carrion

Life Span: 20 to 30 years

IUCN Red List: Near Threatened

As the largest native lizard in North America, the Gila monster has a pretty bad reputation—it was infamous as a dangerous killer in the Wild West. Back then, people believed that the Gila monster expelled its bodily waste through its mouth! An Arizona rancher by the name of Walter Vail supposedly died after being bitten by a Gila in 1890; Vail had to cut off his own finger in order to get away. That same year, a newspaper called the *Arizona Star* warned readers that the monster's bite "is very poisonous and always fatal."

None of those cowboy legends are true. First, Vail lived some 16 years after his Gila encounter; he was ultimately done in by a streetcar. Second, while it's true that the Gila's venom is potent, the lizard doesn't produce enough of the stuff to kill a healthy adult. Finally, Gila monsters expel their waste from their back ends, the same way most animals do.

That said, you do not want to get bitten by a Gila monster! When provoked, the lizard's jaws clamp down, hanging on as it pumps venom into the bite. Wildlife educator Coyote Peterson described his Gila monster bite as akin to "hot lava coursing through my veins."

Gila monsters don't want to deal with humans and spend much of their lives underground. The vast majority of Gila bites are on people's fingers and hands. That suggests all you need to do to avoid being attacked is to simply not put your hand near its weird purple mouth.

KING COBRA

Scientific Name:
Ophiophagus hannah

Range: Southern Asia, especially India and Thailand

Diet: Mainly other snakes

Life Span: 20 years

IUCN Red List: Vulnerable

We mentioned earlier that a threatened black mamba can raise about a third of its body up off the ground, and that's true of other snakes as well. But the king cobra grows as long as 18 feet (5.5 m) from head to tail. In theory, a very angry king cobra could tower *over* your head. Yikes!

But hopefully you'll get out of their way before this happens. King cobras let people know to "back off" by making a warning noise that's more of a low growl than a hiss—it's a bit of a rumbling sound, like an angry dog. They tend to be very shy animals, attacking humans only if absolutely necessary. They only kill about five humans per year—far less than many other, more aggressive types of snakes.

Like other cobras, the king cobra has ribs in its neck that it can stretch out, creating that "hood" effect that the cobras are famous for. King cobras would rather scare off a threat than fight—and considering the fact that their bite contains enough neurotoxin to kill 20 people, that's probably just as well.

KOMODO DRAGON

Scientific Name:
Varanus komodoensis

Range: Indonesia

Diet: Pigs, deer, cattle, carrion, other dragons

Life Span: Males can live as long as 60 years; females only live roughly 30 years.

IUCN Red List:
Vulnerable

The world's largest lizard rules Indonesian islands such as Komodo (thus their name), Rintja, and Padar. Indigenous people refer to them as "land crocodiles."

Komodo dragons grow to about 10 feet (3 m) long and can weigh as much as 300 pounds (135 kg). They are fierce predators with a strong sense of smell and good eyesight in daytime. Their strong jaws can unhinge, enabling them to attack prey far larger than themselves.

There are not many documented cases of humans being killed by Komodo dragons, but it does happen. In 2013 an 8-year-old boy visiting a park on Komodo went into the bushes to urinate and was attacked by a hungry dragon. The boy's family managed to get him to safety, but the boy died soon after.

The cause of the boy's death was probably not the bite itself, but the venom left behind. Komodos are one of the only venomous lizards—their saliva prevents blood from clotting.

But as we see over and over, humans present a bigger problem for the dragons than the other way around. Their numbers are dwindling, primarily due to illegal hunting and habitat loss. The worst problem Komodo dragons present to locals—which, let's admit, is not great—is their fondness for digging up graves to eat the corpses inside.

DINING WITH DRAGONS

Komodo stomachs expand so much that they can eat 80 percent of their body weight in a single sitting—they can go for about a month between meals. But all that extra weight in the stomach can really slow a dragon down. So when they are threatened, they throw up everything they've eaten recently. This helps them make a quicker getaway: once they've vomited out their lunch, they can run at about 20 mph (32 kph) for short periods.

Komodos are not picky eaters—they'll consume pretty much anything, alive or dead. That includes body parts like bones and hooves, and it also includes other Komodo dragons. Baby dragons spend much of their young lives in trees, simply to avoid their cannibalistic family members. Just about the only thing Komodos won't eat is **dung**. That's why young dragons roll around in their own mess—to protect themselves from older Komodos.

SNAPPING TURTLES

Assuming you're reading this book from the safety of a library in North America, the likelihood of you having a king cobra encounter is vanishingly small. Even your chance of being attacked by a Florida alligator is only 1 in 2.4 million. As dangerous as these reptiles may be in *theory*, they pose little or no threat to you in *reality*. For a more realistic chill up your spine, let's turn our attention to two ill-tempered species of freshwater snapping turtle.

ALLIGATOR SNAPPING TURTLE

Scientific Name: *Macrochelys temminckii*

Range: Southeastern United States

Diet: Fish, frogs, crustaceans

Life Span: About 70 years in captivity; possibly far longer in wild

IUCN Red List: Least Concern

With its plated shell, the alligator snapping turtle looks like a distant cousin of the stegosaurus. These are the largest turtles in North America, and among the largest in the world—males weigh about 175 pounds (80 kg) on average.

Alligator snapping turtles are ambush predators, lying in wait on the muddy bottom and grabbing prey with their powerful jaws. They have a small, fleshy appendage in their mouths that looks a bit like a worm. The turtle uses the appendage as a lure, enticing fish, frogs, and crustaceans to wander into the turtle's mouth, and to their doom.

Although they look threatening—especially with their gaping jaws hanging open, waiting for prey—alligator snapping turtles are more threatened than threatening. Asian markets prize them for their meat.

COMMON SNAPPING TURTLE

Scientific Name:
Chelydra serpentine

Range: North America

Diet: Fish, frogs, crustaceans

Life Span: 47 years

IUCN Red List: Least Concern

True to its name, common snapping turtles can be found all over North America: anywhere east of the Rocky Mountains, as far north as Saskatchewan, and all the way down to the Gulf of Mexico. They like wetlands like marshes and swamps, but they'll also live in lakes and slow-moving rivers. In the wild, common snapping turtles can weigh up to 75 pounds (34 kg), although the neighborhood of about 35 pounds (15 kg) is more typical.

Common snapping turtles don't lie around in the mud, waiting for lunch to pass by. Instead they patrol the waters, actively hunting down their prey. Their powerful jaws are designed for chopping—they can chomp down on two fish at once if need be. They can easily remove your fingers or toes, so steer clear.

CHECK IT OUT!

Use the Internet to find out what dangerous reptiles live in your area. Are there snakes, snapping turtles, or even alligators? What advice do experts give on how to stay safe around these creatures? Look up some tips and turn them into a poster.

SPITTING COBRAS

Of the 30 species of cobra, about a third are "spitters," meaning that they're able to fire jets of venom at their prey. Herpetologists refer to spitting as a "long-range" strategy, in contrast to biting, which is clearly a close-range technique.

Interestingly, the venom of spitting cobras tends to be different than the venom of non-spitting cobras. Unlike nonspitting cobras, which rely on neurotoxins, spitting cobras rely more on cytotoxins, which cause immediate tissue damage. Spitting cobras are expert marksmen—they aim their venom directly at the eyes of their antagonist, and researchers have found that they hit their target almost every single time.

SNAKE VENOMS

There are nearly two dozen different types of toxins that can be present in snake venom. No venomous snake has them all, but most have a combination of several. Snakes venoms are divided into several groups, depending on what part of the body they injure. Neurotoxins, which damage the nervous system and brain, are found in the venom of the king cobra, the black mamba, and others. Hemotoxins, which damage the heart and circulatory system, are found in the venom of boomslangs, vipers, and others. Cytotoxins and myotoxins, which damage muscles and other body tissues, are found in the venom of rattlesnakes, among many others.

MOZAMBIQUE SPITTING COBRA

Scientific Name:
Naja mossambica

Range: Southern Africa

Diet: Frogs, birds, insects, small mammals, other snakes

Life Span: About 15–20 years

IUCN Red List: Not assessed

The Mozambique spitting cobra is common throughout southern Africa. It's on the smaller side (about 3 feet [1 m] long), but its venom can cause severe tissue damage and blindness if it gets into a victim's eyes.

Mozambique spitting cobra

ASHE'S SPITTING COBRA

Scientific Name:
Naja ashei

Range: Eastern and northeastern Africa

Diet: Frogs, birds, insects, small mammals, other snakes

Life Span: not known

IUCN Red List: Not assessed

The largest spitting cobra, called Ashe's spitting cobra in honor of the herpetologist (and snake farmer!) James Ashe, was discovered in Kenya in 2004. It grows as long as 9 feet (2.7 m) and produces more venom than any other spitting cobra.

TAIPAN

Three of the world's most deadly snakes are unique to Australia—together, these slithering death machines make up the taipan family. But of the three, there's one we don't know very much about. The desert taipan was only discovered in 2006 and has yet to be thoroughly studied.

INLAND (OR WESTERN) TAIPAN

Scientific Name: *Oxyuranus microlepidotus*

Range: Central and eastern Australia

Diet: Rats and mice, other small animals, small birds

Life Span: About 10 years

IUCN Red List: Least Concern

In the land down under, the inland taipan is simply called "the fierce snake." Australians are not known for their timid personalities, so when they refer to something as "fierce," it's safe to assume they aren't kidding around.

The inland taipan makes its home on Australia's heat-blasted plains, where it hides in the cracked ground by day and hunts for rats by night. The Australia Zoo, located in the prime taipan territory of Queensland, declares—a bit proudly?!—that inland taipan venom is "unequalled in toxicity amongst any snake anywhere in the world." The venom is so powerful that one bite could, in theory, kill a hundred adults.

Fortunately, the fierce snake doesn't present itself to humans very often. It was first identified in 1879, and then wasn't seen again for almost a hundred years. And when a tour guide accidentally discovered a fierce snake in the 1960s, it tried to kill him.

COASTAL TAIPAN

Scientific Name:
Oxyuranus scutellatus

Range: Eastern and northeastern coasts of Australia; a subspecies also lives in southern New Guinea.

Diet: Rats and mice, birds, and other small, warm-blooded animals

Life Span: 10–15 years

IUCN Red List: Least Concern

Some Australians argue for the inland taipan as the continent's most lethal snake. But the coastal taipan also has a fan base. While its venom is "only" the third most lethal in the world, that's more than deadly enough! The neurotoxins in taipan venom cause convulsions, internal bleeding, paralysis, and organ damage. Until the antivenom was invented in 1956, the bite of a coastal taipan was almost invariably fatal.

The coastal taipan encounters more humans than its inland cousin, mostly due to its fondness for hanging out in sugarcane fields. Greater opportunity combined with a nervous disposition has painful results: the coastal taipan bites far more humans than the fierce snake does.

VIPERS

Rattlesnakes, copperheads, and water moccasins are all members of the viper family, so they share certain key characteristics. Most importantly, they are all venomous, with hinged fangs sitting on each side of their upper jaws. The fangs are hollow, serving as ideal delivery systems for vipers to **envenomate** their victims. It's true that their venom is not necessarily as lethal as some other snakes, but those hollow fangs deliver a great deal of it in a very short period of time.

Vipers are ambush predators, and their coloring helps them blend in with their surroundings. Unlike cobras, which rise up and attack from a vertical position, vipers remain lower to the ground and attack horizontally.

RUSSELL'S VIPER

Scientific Name:
Daboia russelii

Range: India, Southern China, Taiwan, Java

Diet: Rodents, lizards

Life Span: About 15 years

IUCN Red List: Least Concern

The Russell's viper is not the biggest snake, and its venom is not the deadliest . . . and yet this snake is blamed for more human attacks than any other in Asia. This killer lives in open spaces such as farmland, leading to frequent collisions with humans. Its venom has a number of unpleasant effects—most especially, it can shut down the kidneys, which frequently causes death.

Russell's viper venom also interferes with the **pituitary gland**, which can cause a sort of puberty reversal, where bite victims lose body hair and become infertile. One estimate suggested that 30,000 people are bitten by Russell's vipers every year.

WESTERN DIAMONDBACK

Scientific Name:
Crotalus atrox

Range: Western
United States

Diet: Mice, rats,
squirrels

Life Span: 20+ years

IUCN Red List: Least
Concern

Diamondback rattlesnakes are not just the bane of cowboys in old-time westerns; they are the most venomous snakes in the United States. The Eastern variety is the largest, sometimes reaching 8 feet (2.5 m) or more. Their venom is a hemotoxin, destroying blood cells and causing extreme pain. Fortunately, antivenom is readily available throughout their ranges, keeping human fatalities low.

They use their famous rattles to warn bystanders that they are annoyed and getting ready to strike. The rattles are made of the same type of protein found in human fingernails. And like fingernails, the rattles break easily but are regrown every time the snake sheds its skin.

EASTERN DIAMONDBACK

Scientific Name:
Crotalus adamanteus

Range: Southeastern
United States

Diet: Rabbits, mice,
rats, squirrels

Life Span: 20+ years

IUCN Red List: Least
Concern

WORDS TO UNDERSTAND

cyanide: an extremely toxic chemical compound

elasmobranchologist: a scientist who studies sharks and rays

immobilize: prevent something from moving

invasive: describes animals or plants that are introduced into an area where they don't belong

predatory: inclined to hurt others for survival

temperate: mild in temperature

topography: the physical features of an area

CHAPTER 3

DANGEROUS SEA CREATURES

Y ou might have heard the claim that "only 5 percent of the ocean has been explored," but this oft-repeated statement isn't precisely true. In fact, scientists *have* mapped the entire ocean.

But there's a catch—these maps are not very detailed. If you're asking whether we have a map of the ocean floor, then the answer is yes. But if you're asking if we have a great understanding of the ocean floor, then the answer, is definitely not. Just because you know the basic **topography** of a place, that doesn't mean you know very much about what is going on there. We may have a better sense of what's happening on the surface of the Moon than we do of what's happening at the very bottom of the ocean.

Nothing inspires fear like the unknown, so it's not surprising that the ocean is home to so many of our most terrifying creatures. From highly venomous snails to giant man-eating sharks, what we've found so far is plenty dangerous!

BOX JELLYFISH

Scientific Name:
Chironex fleckeri

Range: Waters of Australia and Southeast Asia

Diet: Fish, crustaceans

Life Span: About 1 year

IUCN Red List: Least Concern

Also known as the sea wasp, the box jellyfish is one of the ocean's deadliest animals. Full-grown box jellyfish are about the size of your head, with as many as 60 stinging tentacles that can grow as long as 9 feet (3 m). The tentacles are armed with a powerful venom that, in high doses, can kill an adult in under three minutes. Victims who receive a lower dose will survive, but they can expect weeks of horrible pain and severe scarring.

Sea wasps aren't just more deadly than the average jellyfish; they're also far more advanced. Box jellyfish have the ability to propel themselves through water, rather than drifting aimlessly the way their relatives do. Remarkably, they also have 24 eyes—six on each side of their box-like body.

However, jellyfish don't have a central nervous system. It's still a mystery as to how box jellies can interpret visual information. But research indicates that the eyes are used for basic navigational tasks, such as making sure they don't stray too far from their home territories. In an article in *Current Biology,* researchers wrote that the box jellyfish "defeats the idea that a central brain is a prerequisite for advanced behavior."

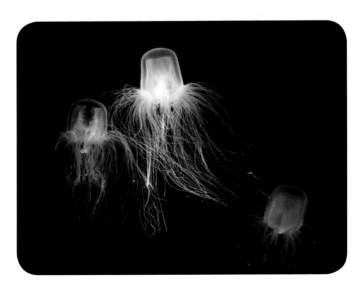

BLUE-RINGED OCTOPUS

In Australia, blue-ringed octopi are credited with more fatalities than sharks!

Scientific Names:
Hapalochlaena lunulata,
Hapalochlaena maculosa,
Hapalochlaena fasciata

Range: Waters of Australia and Southeast Asia

Diet: Crabs, shrimp, small fish

Life Span: About 2 years

IUCN Red List: Not assessed

It sounds like a riddle from a grim children's story: *It bites you with its beak and poisons you with its venom . . . what is it?* The answer is the adorably deadly blue-ringed octopus.

There are at least three species of blue-ringed octopus (probably more, but their status is uncertain) in the tide pools and coral reefs of the Indo-Pacific. Primarily they live around Australia, but the greater blue-ringed octopus can also be found off Indonesia, the Philippines, and Sri Lanka. They spit a powerful poison called tetrodotoxin, which is about a thousand times more powerful than **cyanide**. The bite tends to be painless, so a victim may not even know he or she has been bitten until it is too late. The toxin causes numbness, paralysis, and respiratory failure. Worst of all, the victim remains fully conscious even when totally paralyzed. But there is no known antivenom; survival depends on getting immediate respiratory care.

BULL SHARK

Scientific Name:
Carcharhinus leucas

Range: Temperate
and tropical waters,
worldwide

Diet: Bony fish, other
sharks

Life Span: About 12
years

IUCN Red List: Near
Threatened

Although great white sharks get all the press,
according to many **elasmobranchologists**, the
real "man-killer" of the shark family is the bull shark.

Bull sharks are classified as medium-sized sharks,
definitely smaller than great whites. That said, at a
maximum size of 11.5 feet (3.5 m) and about 500

pounds (230 kg), bull sharks aren't exactly petite, either. But what really makes bull sharks dangerous to humans is proximity. They patrol the shallow water of tropical shorelines, precisely where humans love to swim.

What's more, bull sharks aren't troubled by freshwater—they have special glands in their tails that keep their bodies salted even when the water around them is not. Consequently, bull sharks don't have to limit their hunting to the ocean—they've been known to hunt in rivers and lakes as well. They've even been spotted leaping up rapids, just like salmon do. Mammoth, human-eating salmon.

THE JERSEY MAN-EATER

In 1916 the eastern United States was swept up in a shark panic. At the time, scientists believed that sharks would never attack humans. They were proved spectacularly wrong during the first two weeks of July, when four people were killed and one injured in multiple shark attacks along the New Jersey shore.

The first victim, Charles Vansant, was swimming in the ocean when he was attacked. Bystanders managed to pull him from the water, but he soon bled to death in the lobby of his hotel. This was followed by an attack along the shore of the town of Spring Lake, and another two attacks in Mattawan Creek, in which two young boys were killed. The location of those attacks is significant, because Mattawan Creek is an inlet of Raritan Bay—not the kind of place you'd see a great white, but a perfect hunting ground for a bull shark.

A variety of sharks were blamed for the attacks, great whites especially. But the exact species of the "Jersey Man-Eater" has never been precisely confirmed. Many people now believe a bull shark is likely the guilty party.

CONE SNAILS

Scientific Names:
Ophiophagus hannah

Range: Red Sea, Indian Ocean, and coasts of Australia and New Zealand, Indonesia, and some African countries

Diet: Sea worms, small fish, other snails

Life Span: Uncertain, estimated 10–20 years

IUCN Red List: Least Concern

As odd as it may sound, cone snails are both **predatory** and carnivorous. There are about 500 different species, and they all compensate for being slow moving by being highly venomous. Cone snails have a tooth that is essentially a tiny, venom-filled harpoon. The snail fires the harpoon at prey to paralyze it, thereby gaining enough time to slowly glide over to its victim and eat it. The tooth itself also gets eaten in the process, but the snail is able to grow a new one, and the cycle begins again.

One type of cone snail that's particularly associated with human fatalities is the geographic cone snail. Although it's small enough to fit in a soup bowl, its venom, called conotoxin, is arguably the most dangerous on Earth. There is no antivenom; the only remedy is to help the victim keep breathing until the poison wears off.

Another highly lethal member of the cone family is the textile cone snail (pictured). It is nicknamed "the cloth of gold," because its patterned shell looks like elaborately woven fabric. Cone snails have long been prized by shell collectors.

Cone venom contains substances called conantokins, which researchers hope can be used as effective medications for people with a wide variety of illnesses, including AIDS, Alzheimer's, and Parkinson's. There's already one painkiller on the market, called ziconotide, that is made from the venom of a species known as the magician's cone snail.

ELECTRIC EEL

Scientific Name:
Electrophorus eletricus

Range: Waters of
South America

Diet: Small fish and
invertebrates

Life Span: Males,
10–15 years; females,
12–22 years

IUCN Red List: Least
Concern

Despite their name, electric eels aren't eels—they are relatives of the catfish. Essentially swimming batteries, electric eels discharge painful amounts of electricity into their prey, which they swallow whole. Their goal is to stun and **immobilize** their dinner, not to kill it. Prey that is accidentally electrocuted won't be eaten.

Electric eels were identified in 1800 by the naturalist Alexander von Humboldt. While traveling in Venezuela, he stepped on one and regretted it. Humboldt wrote that he experienced "a violent pain in the knees and in almost every joint." He also saw something amazing: electric eels leaping out of the water to attack his horses.

The sight was so amazing, in fact, that almost no one believed Humboldt's story. It wasn't until 200 years later that eel expert Ken Catania proved that electric eels can, in fact, jump out of the water. Not only that, the action of leaping increases the amount of electricity the eel can deliver.

The discharge of an electric eel could theoretically kill a human, but the most likely outcome of an eel encounter is intense-but-survivable pain. The biggest risk is that the person drowns after being shocked.

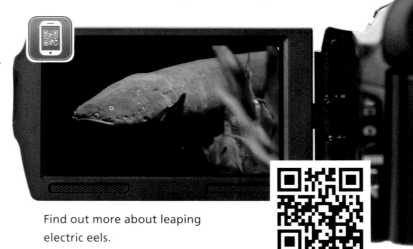

Find out more about leaping electric eels.

GREAT BARRACUDA

Scientific Name: *Sphyraena barracuda*

Range: Warm waters, including the Gulf of Mexico, Caribbean, Mediterranean, and Red Seas, and off the coast of South America

Diet: Fish

Life Span: About 14 years in captivity

IUCN Red List: Least Concern

Picture yourself scuba diving in the warm coastal waters of Rio de Janeiro, or perhaps in the Mediterranean Sea. You glance to one side, and right there beside you is a giant fish, about 5 feet (1.5 m) long, with a mouthful of razors. It's a giant barracuda. You gingerly swim away, but when you look back, there it is again. It isn't doing much of anything—in fact, it's barely moving. But it is following you, watching your every move.

POISON FISH?

You may have heard the rumor that barracuda are poisonous to eat. That's about half true. In their natural state, barracuda are not poisonous at all, and some would say they are downright tasty! However, some waters have a type of plankton called dinoflagellates. The plankton is harmless to sea creatures, but it causes a nasty type of food poisoning in humans. Small fish eat dinoflagellates, and then those fish are eaten by larger ones such as the barracuda. Over time, that poison builds up in the flesh of the big fish.

Not all barracuda are full of toxic dinoflagellates. The problem is, you can't be 100 percent sure whether any given fish is contaminated or not. All in all, it's better to stay away from eating barracuda and just admire them for their . . . um . . . beauty?

The great barracuda and its 27 species of relatives have been creeping out divers and fishermen for generations. Barracudas are ambush predators—they wait quietly in the water and then spring out to attack prey without warning. Small fish are swallowed whole, while larger ones are torn apart by the barracuda's powerful jaws.

Experts say they are not really looking to attack humans; their bad reputation seems to rest mostly on their unpleasant appearance and number of alarmingly sharp teeth. But barracudas *are* curious about people and will follow them around in the water, which can lead to some unpleasant and occasionally bloody interactions. Trouble occurs when, for example, a barracuda and a spear fisherman both go for the same prey at the same time. There also have been reports of barracuda leaping out of the water after some prey and ending up biting a human instead.

GREAT WHITE SHARK

Scientific Name:
Carcharodon carcharias

Range: Warm waters all over the world; along coasts of the United States, as well as parts of South America, Europe, Africa, South Asia, and Australia

Diet: Fish and marine mammals like seals and otters

Life Span: Estimated at 70 years

IUCN Red List: Vulnerable

It's one of the few animals to have its own theme song—that unmistakable *dun nah . . . dun nah, dun nah, dun nah . . .* from the movie *Jaws*. The 1975 horror classic features a killer great white stalking the fictional town of Amity, Massachusetts.

Despite their cinematic fame, there's a lot we don't know about great white sharks. Even their size is debated: the general consensus seems to be they grow to about 19 or 20 feet (6 m) long. We also know they are fast! They scan the water for prey, which they are able to smell from about 2 miles (3 km) away. Once they've identified something tasty, they pursue their meals at about 24 mph (38 kph). With as many as 300 teeth arranged in multiple rows, they can easily kill with a single bite.

The number of great white attacks on humans tends to be exaggerated. Perhaps that's because when they do occur, the results can be extremely grim. While *Jaws* isn't a true story, it did come alarmingly close to reality in August 2018, when there were several great white attacks, one fatal, in the waters off Plymouth, Massachusetts. In case you're wondering—yes, Plymouth authorities did learn from the mayor of Amity's mistake, and they quickly closed the beaches.

LIONFISH

Scientific Name: *Pterois volitans*

Range: Native to the Indian and South Pacific Oceans; introduced in the American Southeast

Diet: Smaller fish

Life Span: 15 years

IUCN Red List: Least Concern

Danger can come in many different forms. The beautiful, venomous lionfish is a rare animal that manages to be dangerous in two ways at the same time.

This carnivorous tropical fish has venom-tipped spines that, while not fatal, are extremely painful to humans. The neurotoxin causes breathing problems and even paralysis in the worst cases.

The second type of danger is less obvious but arguably worse. Lionfish are popular in home aquariums, which is fine until they are freed from their tanks and left to breed unchecked. The National Oceanographic and Atmospheric Administration (NOAA) reports that people have been releasing lionfish into Atlantic waters for decades, and now the fish is well-established in the Gulf of Mexico and along the southeastern Atlantic coast.

Hungry lionfish present challenging competition for native predators and reduce the amount of food available. Lionfish can eat up to 90 percent of their body weight every day.

One way to address this problem would be for humans to develop a taste for lionfish. Their flesh is said to be similar to popular edible fish, while containing even more nutrients. Save a grouper, eat a lionfish!

Find out more about **invasive** lionfish.

PORTUGUESE MAN-OF-WAR

Scientific Name:
Physalia physalis

Range: Temperate waters of the Atlantic, Caribbean, Indian Ocean, and parts of the Pacific Ocean

Diet: Small fish

Life Span: Unknown

IUCN Red List: Not assessed

The Portuguese man-of-war (or man o' war) is a trick bag of a beast. It looks like it's made of glass, but it isn't. It looks like it's a jellyfish, but it isn't. It looks like it's just one animal, but it isn't that, either!

The Portuguese man-of-war is a *siphonophore*, which means that it's actually multiple creatures (called *zooids*) together in a colony. They drift by means of a gas-filled bladder, which has a fin-like part at the top that acts as a sail. Dangling below—as far down as 165 feet (50 m)—are venomous tentacles that trap and paralyze small fish. Once the prey is trapped, the man-of-war uses chemicals to liquefy and consume its meal.

Man-of-wars do not present any liquefaction danger to humans, which is a relief! However, the venom in their tentacles causes extreme pain and, in rare cases, even death. Toxicology analysis suggests that the man-of-war's venom is

This extraordinary little beast is called a blue dragon sea slug. Blue dragons only grow to be about an inch long. They not only feed on Portuguese man-of-wars, but they also harvest the venom for their own use. In 2018 a number of blue dragons stung people at Cape Canaveral, Florida, and the venom was identical to that of a Portuguese man-of-war.

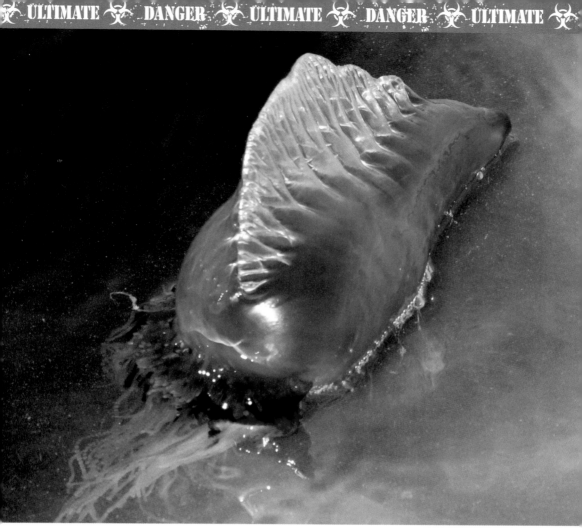

similar to that found in snakes. While it's not nearly as powerful as, say, the venom of the blue-ringed octopus, you still don't want to get anywhere near it.

That brings us to the final item in the man-of-war's bag of tricks. Because they don't have much control over where the tide takes them, it is not unusual to see one washed up on a beach. In fact, it's not that unusual to see as many as a thousand of them washed up; man-of-wars tend to drift together in groups known as *legions*. They may look quite helpless, lying there on the sand all deflated and scraggly. But beware—a beached man-of-war can sting you just like a swimming one can. Steer clear!

PUFFERFISH

Scientific Names: *Takifugu rubripes,* and more than 100 others

Range: Northwestern Pacific Ocean, around Japan, South Korea, and parts of China

Diet: Algae, small invertebrates

Life Span: 10 years

IUCN Red List: Near Threatened

Pufferfish, also called blowfish, have the unique ability to fill themselves up with water when they're threatened. Biologists speculate that pufferfish developed this defensive ability because they just aren't great swimmers. Since gracefully darting away from predators was never going to be an option, they needed some other way to defend themselves.

The internal organs of the pufferfish contain tetrodotoxin, a uniquely deadly compound—far more dangerous to humans than cyanide. Tetrodotoxin not only makes pufferfish dangerous for predators to eat, but it also makes them taste terrible.

How odd, then, that pufferfish are considered to be one of the world's great delicacies. In Japan, where pufferfish are called *fugu*, master chefs very carefully remove the poisonous organs so they can cook the delicate flesh that remains. Chefs must train for 3 years and pass a special test before they are allowed to prepare fugu; the failure rate on the fugu test is around 65 percent.

Fugu is a dinner for daredevils. It's served grilled, seared, boiled, as sashimi (raw and sliced very thin), and in many other preparations. A handful of people die every year from accidental tetrodotoxin exposure. However, it's important to note that the majority of fugu fatalities occur when people try to prepare the pufferfish on their own. Restaurants have far better survival rates. Nevertheless, fugu is the one dish that the emperor of Japan is not allowed to eat, for his own safety.

STONEFISH

Scientific Name: *Actinopyga lecanora*

Range: Western Pacific and Indian Oceans

Diet: Small fish

Life Span: 10 years

IUCN Red List: Data deficient

The most deadly venomous fish on Earth is the stonefish. Unlike many creatures in this chapter, the stonefish does not use its poison for hunting. The venom is purely defensive, and it is kept in little sacs connected to the spikes running along its back. If you step on a stone fish, the spikes function like a needle—the pressure from your foot compresses the venom sacs, sending the poison into your foot. The pain is said to be almost unbearable, causing breathing problems, heart failure, and death.

Stonefish live in what's called the *intertidal zone*—the part of the beach that's covered with water during high tides but exposed to air during low tides. To survive, stonefish are able to hold water in their gills; they can be exposed to air for several hours and not suffer any ill consequences. Unfortunately, people walking along the beach can suffer extremely ill consequences if they don't watch where they are going! By one estimate, as many as a thousand of people a year are stung by stonefish—just along the coast of Australia alone. Dr. Simon Jensen, who works at a hospital in Queensland, told a reporter in 2018 that "it's not uncommon for people to come out of the water screaming in pain."

In order to make the antidote, a stonefish needs to be caught and . . . wait for it . . . milked. A specialist known as a venomologist removes and collects the poison, which is sent to a lab where it can be used to create an antivenom.

WORDS TO UNDERSTAND

hominid: a primate that is an ancestor of humans

ornithologist: someone who studies birds

raptor: a category of birds that includes hawks and eagles

CHAPTER 4

DANGEROUS BIRDS

I n August 1961, the seaside town of Capitola, California, was attacked by thousands of sooty shearwaters, a type of seabird common to that part of Monterey Bay. Some crashed into buildings, some had seizures, and some fell dead from the sky. According to the local newspaper, "dead and stunned seabirds littered the streets and roads." The incident became part of the inspiration for Alfred Hitchcock's film *The Birds*.

Eventually, the source of the problem was traced to a deadly neurotoxin that had started in the water and worked its way up the food chain until finally reaching the birds. As it turned out, the sooty shearwaters were not "attacking" Capitola after all—they were just disoriented and sick.

In general, birds don't pose much of a threat to humans. And when they do, it's usually by accident, such as what occurred in Capitola, or what happened in 2009 when a commercial airplane crash-landed in the Hudson River after an unpleasant encounter with a flock of Canada geese. But there are a few birds that can do considerable damage to humans if we're not careful.

AFRICAN CROWNED EAGLE

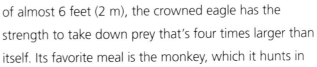

Scientific Names:
Stephanoaetus coronatus

Range: Central and southeastern Africa

Diet: Monkeys

Life Span: 15 years

IUCN Red List: Near Threatened

One of the continent's largest **raptors**, the African crowned eagle has, perhaps unfairly, a murderous reputation.

With a wingspan of almost 6 feet (2 m), the crowned eagle has the strength to take down prey that's four times larger than itself. Its favorite meal is the monkey, which it hunts in the trees of Central Africa's forests and wetlands. When the eagle encounters a troop of monkeys, it lands in the branches above them and gradually inches downward. When the eagle gets close enough, it drops down, grabbing an unlucky monkey, taking it down, too. On the ground, the eagle breaks the monkey's spine with its talons, dismembers it, and carries the pieces back to its nest.

That's grim enough, but rumors persist that pieces of young *children* have been found in crowned eagle nests. It's important to note that this has not been proven definitively, so the African crowned eagle's reputation as a child-killer may be entirely unfair.

That said, workers in a quarry in Taung, South Africa, found a skull that was later identified as a 3-year-old *Australopithecus africanus*, an early **hominid** ancestor. The skull had markings around the eyes suggesting it was killed by an eagle. Interestingly, when this discovery was made in 1924, it was assumed that an eagle could never kill a child that would have weighed around 25 pounds (11 kg). Therefore, researchers theorized that our tiny ancestor was killed by some large predator, and then the eagle took the skull later. We've since learned that crowned eagles routinely kill monkeys that weigh as much or more. This makes it quite plausible that the "Taung Child" was, indeed, killed by an eagle. It also, alas, makes it plausible that crowned eagles might have taken other small children as well.

AFRICAN SPUR-WINGED GOOSE

Scientific Name:
Plectropterus gambensis

Range: Central and southern Africa

Diet: Plants, seeds, and fruit; small fish; insects

Life Span: 25 years

IUCN Red List: Least Concern

The African spur-winged goose is the continent's largest water bird. It's dangerous on two different fronts.

First, the geese have bony spikes, or spurs, at the spot where their wings bend—what **ornithologists** call their "wrists." These very sharp spurs are used as weapons against prey, or, in certain situations, against other geese or humans. Like most geese, spur-winged geese are fiercely territorial and can get aggressive, particularly if they are defending their young.

The second threat involves the African spur-winged goose's diet. Primarily, these geese eat water plants, but they are also happy to dine on insects. The problem is that one of their favorites is the blister beetle, which secretes a toxic substance called cantharidin. Cantharidin burns the skin (thus the "blister" in the beetle's name), and it is poisonous in large doses. The geese aren't much bothered by cantharidin, but over time, the poison builds up in their flesh, making the African spur-winged goose a potentially deadly meal for humans.

CASSOWARY

Scientific Name:
Casuarius casuarius

Range: Australia; parts of Indonesia and Papua New Guinea

Diet: Grass, fruit, leaves, snails, frogs, insects, mice, carrion

Life Span: 60 years in captivity; unknown in wild

IUCN Red List: Least Concern

The southern cassowary is the largest and most common type of this flightless, forest-dwelling bird. (The other two types are the northern cassowary and the dwarf cassowary). Unlike most birds, where the males are larger and more colorful, female cassowaries are the larger and prettier. They can grow to over 6 feet (3 m) tall, and weigh as much as 130 pounds (nearly 60 kg).

Cassowaries are extremely shy, and they are fast—traveling at 31 mph (50 kph) when necessary. They're good at hiding in the forests where they live, so they haven't been as well studied as some other animals. But when confrontation is necessary, cassowaries are fierce fighters—they will charge and kick an opponent, potentially causing bone fractures, intestinal bruising, or worse. Cassowaries also have three toes on each foot, and the middle toe serves as a dagger that can be used to slash its prey. In 1926 an Australian teenager tried to kill a cassowary that had wandered onto his property, and instead the cassowary slit open his jugular vein, causing the young man's death shortly after.

While death-by-cassowary is a very rare occurrence, cassowary attacks are more common. About 70 percent of the time, the attacks are related to humans feeding the birds when

Find out more about cassowaries.

they should not do so. What seems to happen is that cassowaries begin to expect that all humans will always offer food. The birds can then get extremely annoyed if no treats are forthcoming.

WORDS TO UNDERSTAND

aposematic: color or markings that warn or repel predators

neurotoxin: poison that affects the brain and nervous system

CHAPTER 5

DANGEROUS AMPHIBIANS

A mphibians are cold-blooded animals that spend the first part of their lives in water and later develop lungs and live on land. The classic example is tadpoles, which start life looking somewhat like fish but grow into frogs and toads.

Whether it's the Geico Gecko, Kermit the Frog, or Mr. Toad from *Wind in the Willows*, amphibians in popular culture aren't particularly threatening. Sometimes they're singing like Michigan J. Frog, other times they're just trying to survive to the end of the game, like the little guy hopping across the street in Frogger. But don't be fooled— certain members of the amphibian family are as dangerous as any sharp-toothed mammal or reptile.

CANE TOAD

Scientific Name:
Rhinella marina

Range: Native to parts of Central and South America, and also to parts of Mexico and the United States; invasive in Australia, Oceania, and parts of the Caribbean

Diet: Beetles, other insects

Life Span: 10 to 15 years

IUCN Red List: Least Concern

The cane toad is common throughout the Americas. It secretes a milky brew of several toxins from glands just above its shoulders. The poison is not terribly dangerous to humans; most of the poisons mentioned throughout this book are far worse.

The danger posed by the cane toad is less about its toxicity and more about its highly unwelcome presence in Australia, where it is doing large amounts of environmental damage. The cane toad was introduced to the Land Down Under in the 1930s; sugarcane plantations were hoping that the toad would help control insects that were destroying the crops. Taken out of its natural habitat, the cane toad had no natural predators. One study estimated there are now some 200 million cane toads in the country.

Predators that do try eating cane toads often end up dead. Crocodiles, lizards, turtles, and certain birds are all falling prey to the cane toad's particular poison. Other birds, meanwhile, such as crimson finches, are experiencing a population increase because their main predators, monitor lizards, are being killed off by the cane toads. Some ecologists in Australia are currently conducting experiments to see how they might train certain predators to avoid the cane toads and thus save their own lives.

Find out more about Australia's struggle with the cane toad.

COLORADO RIVER TOAD

Scientific Names:
Incilius alvarius

Range: Mexico and Western United States

Diet: Beetles and other insects, small frogs

Life Span: 10 to 20 years

IUCN Red List: Least Concern

Also known as the Sonoran Desert toad, this large toad produces a **neurotoxin** in glands located between its eyes and in its legs. The poison causes diarrhea, vomiting, and foaming at the mouth. It is rarely fatal to humans, but it's extremely dangerous to smaller animals such as dogs. Media in the southwestern U.S. states regularly warn pet owners about keeping their animals away from areas where the toads are common.

The Colorado River toad is probably most famous for its association with the practice of "toad licking," in which people—yes—lick the toad in order to ingest a small amount of the neurotoxin. The poison has chemical similarities to the psychedelic drug LSD, and it can cause hallucinations that last anywhere from 10 minutes to about an hour.

Some indigenous people in the Southwest include toad poison as part of their religious rituals. But it's important to remember that there is no dosage information on a toad! Ingesting too much of the poison can cause an overdose and even death in people with weak cardiac systems. There is no antitoxin to counteract the poison.

POISON DART FROGS

Many animals have evolved coloring that helps them blend into their environments. But poison dart frogs have gone in the opposite direction—rather than attempting to blend in, these small South American frogs use **aposematic** coloration to warn predators to stay away. In fact, the more brightly colored these frogs are, the more dangerous they are. Their poison comes from their diet—they eat small insects, which themselves eat poisonous plants, and in that way the toxins move from the plants to the frogs.

DYEING POISON DART FROG

Scientific Name:
Dendrobates tinctorius

Range: Northern parts of South America

Diet: Small insects

Life Span: 4–6 years; 10 years in captivity

IUCN Red List: Not evaluated

This toxic species of frog lives in the forests of Suriname, Guyana, and Brazil. Dyeing poison dart frogs come in a wide variety of colors—many are mainly black, but there are also blue, purple, yellow, and white ones. Due to the many colors they display, there's a legend that parrots get their amazing coloration from eating the frogs.

STRAWBERRY POISON DART FROG

Scientific Name: *Oophaga pumilio*

Range: Central America, especially Costa Rica, Nicaragua, Panama

Diet: Small insects

Life Span: 17 years in captivity

IUCN Red List: Least Concern

This is the most poisonous of the Oophaga family of poison frogs—there are eight other types, including the polka dot, the granular, and the harlequin. The strawberry poison dart frog is also one of the more popular types to keep as a pet. Because the frogs get their toxins from what they eat, a frog that doesn't eat poisonous beetles grows up to be a nonpoisonous version of the frog.

GOLDEN POISON DART FROG

Scientific Name: *Phyllobates terribilis*

Range: West coast of Colombia

Diet: Small insects

Life Span: 20 years in captivity

IUCN Red List: Endangered

There are many types of poisonous frogs, but the golden poison dart frog is the most dangerous of all. Although it's only an inch or two long at most (about 3–5 cm), its poison could kill 10 adults. It's roughly 20 times more poisonous than its poisonous relatives.

An indigenous group in Colombia called the Emberá used the golden dart frogs' toxin to make their blow darts more deadly. The process of acquiring poison dart frog toxin is unpleasant for everyone involved—most especially the frogs themselves. The Emberá would capture the frogs and push sharp sticks down their throats and out their legs. Whatever the method, the idea was to make the frogs upset, causing them to sweat out their poison.

SERIES GLOSSARY OF KEY TERMS

anaphylaxis: a type of severe and potentially fatal allergic reaction

antibiotic: any of a class of drugs that can inhibit or destroy microorganisms that cause illness

arid: having little or no rain

asphyxiation: to deprive one of air; to choke or suffocate an animal to death

benign: not harmful

blunt-force trauma: an injury caused by colliding with something

bona fide: genuine, real

booby traps: seemingly harmless objects that contain an explosive device designed to kill or maim

camouflage: a defense mechanism animals use to blend into their surroundings to escape predators

cannibalism: the practice of eating the flesh of one's own species

cartel: an association of suppliers

class action: a type of lawsuit filed on behalf of a large group or "class" of people

claustrophobic: extremely fearful of confined places

climate change: a change in global or regional climate patterns attributed largely to the effects of greenhouse gases, such as carbon dioxide

cyanide: an extremely toxic chemical compound

deforestation: the destruction of forests by humans

degenerative: wasting away

demilitarized zone: an area between warring countries that is devoid of military installations, based on treaties or other agreements

destitute: extremely poor

disoriented: confused

emaciated: dangerously thin, due to lack of food

endurance: able to withstand something difficult

entomologist: a scientist who studies insects

envenomate: the process by which venom is injected by means of a bite or sting

exploited: taken advantage of

extrajudicial: beyond or outside the legal system

fire suppressant: a chemical that can extinguish a fire

flotsam: bits and pieces of debris floating on the water

frostbite: injury caused to body tissue by exposure to extreme cold

genotoxic: describes something that can cause genetic mutations

gore: to stab with a horn or tusk

hypothermia: abnormally low body temperature

insurgency: rebellion

inundated: flooded, swamped

malaria: a serious and sometimes fatal infectious disease that is spread by certain types of mosquitoes

ordnance: military explosives, such as missiles and bombs

pathogen: bacterium, virus, or microorganism that can cause disease

perilous: dangerous

pheromone: a chemical substance produced and released into the environment by an organism, which affects the behavior of others in its species

predators: animals that prey on others

regulations: rules enforced by the government, including governing the way industries behave

sinkhole: an opening in the ground caused by a variety of factors, including erosion

squeamish: easily nauseated or disgusted

stamina: the ability to withstand continued physical activity

torrential: relentless rain

treacherous: extremely risky

venerate: worship

vernacular: everyday language

FURTHER READING AND INTERNET RESOURCES

BOOKS

Claybourne, Anna. *100 Deadliest Things on the Planet.* New York: Scholastic, 2012.

Derrick, Stuart, and Charlotte Goddard. *The World's Strangest Predators.* New York: Lonely Planet Kids, 2018.

Harvey, Derek. *Nature's Deadliest Creatures: A Visual Encyclopedia.* New York: DK Children, 2018.

Kavanaugh, James. *Australia's Dangerous Animals.* Dunedin, FL: Waterford Press, 2015.

Skerry, Brian. *The Ultimate Book of Sharks.* Washington, DC: National Geographic Partners, 2018.

Ultimate Predator-pedia. Washington, DC: National Geographic Books, 2018.

WEBSITES

BBC News: "What Are the World's Most Dangerous Animals?"

https://www.bbc.com/news/world-36320744

A fact-filled introduction to some of the top killers.

IUCN Red List

https://newredlist.iucnredlist.org

The International Union for Conservation of Nature hosts a massive, easy-to-search database with comprehensive information about the world's animals.

"Perfect Beast: Dangerous Animals"

http://www.natgeotv.com/int/perfect-beast/galleries/dangerous-animals

Photo galleries with amazing images of dangerous creatures, hosted by *National Geographic*.

VIDEO CLIPS

CHAPTER 1

This video of Cape buffalo in action proves how dangerous they can be.

http://x-qr.net/1K2y

CHAPTER 2

Find out what it's like to die of a boomslang bite.

http://x-qr.net/1KdX

CHAPTER 3

Find out more about leaping electric eels.

http://x-qr.net/1KEn

Find out more about invasive lionfish.

http://x-qr.net/1J8F

CHAPTER 4

Find out more about cassowaries.

http://x-qr.net/1Jq8

CHAPTER 5

Find out more about Australia's struggle with the cane toad.

http://x-qr.net/1K4p

INDEX

AUTHOR'S BIOGRAPHY

H.W. Poole is a writer of books for young people, including *The Big World of Fun Facts* (Lonely Planet Kids) and the sets *Childhood Fears and Anxieties, Families Today,* and *Mental Illnesses and Disorders* (Mason Crest). She created the *Horrors of History* series (Charlesbridge) and the *Ecosystems* series (Facts On File). She was coauthor and editor of *The History of the Internet* (ABC-CLIO), which won the 2000 American Library Association RUSA award.

PHOTO CREDITS